ETERNAL LOVE

By
Jaydeep Khot

First Published, 2016
Printed in India
Printed by: Dhote Offset Printers

ISBN : 978-9-35201-704-1
Editing: Wordit CDE
Cover Design:

The Write Place
A Publishing Initiative by Crossword Bookstores Ltd.
Paradigm, A-Wing, 1st Floor, Mindspace, Link Road,
Malad West, Mumbai 400064, India.

Web: www.TheWritePlace.in
Facebook: TheWritePlace.in
Twitter: @WritePlacePub
Instagram: @WritePlacePub

TABLE OF CONTENTS

ACKNOWLEDGMENTS

I would like to thank

My father, Surendra Khot.
Who supported and encouraged me to become a writer.

My mother, Puja Khot,
Who made me love the person I am.

My sister, Tanvi Khot,
Who has always been my best friend.

My friends, who are my extended family,
Drishti Jain, Shristi Tibrewal, Prerna Gaurisaria, Shubham Munot, Aastha Singhania, Anish Prabhu, Divyaj Podar, Shreya Saraf, Aditi Maheshwari, Mukta Tak, Arnav Tulsian, Alisha Sheikh, Akhil Malkani.

Rhythm resort, lonavala.
It's library had comfortable thinking chairs and soothing music which helped me write with ease.

AUTHOR BIO

Jaydeep Khot is a 21 year old writer.
He is an alumnus of Narsee Monjee College of Commerce and Economics.
He is also a Final CA student.
His favorite subjects are history, economics and psychology.
Writing is his passion.

PART 1
LOVE CHRONICLES

LOVE AT FIRST SIGHT

They saw each other for the first time,
Their eyes led the way to their hearts.

It was Valentine's Day,
Both of them were without dates.

Their eyes locked together;
And soon, their hearts would too.

Love birds all around,
Made them edgy, a little nervous…

Finally, he approached her,
He smiled; her face lit up.

They said their first words,
But it felt like they knew each other forever.

As they exchanged numbers,
The thrill in the air was unmistakable.

He looked at her when she wasn't looking,
Her eyes were as deep as an ocean.

He was in love, he knew.
But what about her?

She admired his charming self,
But was unsure all the same.

The first impression would last forever,
Their story was eternal.

To be written in the golden pages of history,
Yet, what would happen next was a mystery.

They departed, exchanging goodbyes;
Only to meet again.

THEY MEET AGAIN

They kept their plan a secret,
Once they decided to see each other again.

It was exciting,
They had never felt this way before.

Time passed slowly,
Their heart beats skipped fast.

Love was overcoming fear,
The right moment was coming near.

They met at her favorite coffee shop,
He couldn't stop admiring her beauty;

They talked, laughed, they shared stories,
Time went by, but neither wanted to leave.

Excuses were thought of and rejected,
Not even one seemed plausible.

Just then, her mother called
She nervously picked up the phone…

And was called back immediately,
There was nothing to be done.

It was urgent,
It couldn't be told over the phone.
He dropped her to her house,
Worried and disturbed, he hugged her before leaving

She waved goodbye and turned;
He waited till he could see her no more.

THE LONG WAIT

He waited for her call,
There was none.

He called and messaged her,
There was no reply.

His worse fears took over his mind,
He felt ignored abandoned, misled...

With each passing day, he grew lonelier,
All he wanted was to hear from her, one the last time.

He started blaming himself,
Wondering where he went wrong.

Life wasn't fair,
He had thought they were perfect.

He had become this attached to her,
In less than 48 hours.

But it was time to convince himself,
That she was gone forever.

He prayed so that he could forget her,
But it was an impossible task.

His love had been defeated,
It was a hard fact to digest.

She was his first love,
Would she also be his last?

HOPE

His phone rang as he was sleeping,
It was her.

He answered immediately,
Her voice was soft and scared.

She asked him to meet,
He simply followed instructions.

But this time
The situation was serious.

She was in tears,
He couldn't bear to see her cry.

He tried to cajole, to wipe them off,
But she resisted.

That's when he understood,
She was hurt more deeply than he knew.

He tried questioning her again,
But she changed the topic.

Instead, she put on a mask—and smiled;
This misled him.

The situation cooled down,
And he dismissed it without another thought.

But he was wrong--terribly wrong,
And unaware of the real situation.

His love was back, that's all he thought,
Hope had helped him win her back.

GAME

It was an important match for him,
He was representing his office.

It was a football match,
He was the main striker.

She was there to cheer on the stands,
As his lucky charm.

His happiness knew no bounds,
Just to have her by his side.

The match began.
He was all charged up.

She gave him strength,
A confidence he never had before.

She was the light,
That removed the darkness from his life.

His teammate gave him a pass,
He took it – and scored.

She smiled at him from the stand,
At that very moment, he knew, she loved him.

He had scored the only goal,
They finally won the match.

He took her out to celebrate,
She met all his teammates.

They had a great time that night,
She felt amazing and her sorrow lessened.

Now, she knew, that he was right for her,
But it was not the right time.

MEMORIES

They shared stories from their past,
Trying to live them again,

She talked about her childhood,
He boasted about his youth.
She loved candies in every flavor,
He loved toy cars of every color.

Both wished they could live each moment again,
But this time, together.

Their love was approaching a deeper stage,
They wanted to be with each other in every age.

Finally, she opened up about her sorrows,
Her eyes brimming over with tears.

He held her hand tightly,
Assuring her that he would always be there.

He could barely sit through her story,
But his heart could feel her pain.

He tried comforting her in whatever way he could,
Making her smile was now his only agenda.

He asked her what he could do,
She told him, never to leave her.

Life was cruel,
But she was so beautiful, he thought.

He could die if she asked,
But he wanted to live with her forever.

He took her hand again and looked into her eyes,
This comforted her – and she smiled.

SOMEDAY

They dreamt of a brighter future,
Someday, they would be together forever.

She engrossed in her paintings,
Him, immersed in his job.

They argued about the names of their kids,
Till date they haven't settled on it.

A future so bright and peaceful,
It would be nothing but joy.

They wanted to set an example,
Which the world would admire and revere;

It was wonderful imagining it,
The little details of their life together.

Their kids going to school,
Learning about values, and about love.

They would be responsible,
Their souls with shine with love and care.

Only if the day was today…
But life was different now, it wasn't perfect.

They prayed every day for their dreams,
All they wanted was to be together.

She felt blessed to have him,
He lacked the words to express his joy.

That day would come soon, they knew.
This was the only thought that kept them going.

ASPIRATIONS

Her passion was in painting,
He wanted to make it big in the city.

Her life was her art,
His life was his work.

Both wanted to reach for the skies,
But their mountains were different.

She took an art class,
He underwent a corporate training program.

Soon, they didn't even have time
To meet each other every day.

Days passed without calls or messages,
They were drifting apart.

Their love grew faint, but they
Were busy working on their dreams.

Their important dream together, however;
It was left unfulfilled.

They were meant to be,
But weren't able to be.

Their paths were different,
And they wouldn't cross each other,

The love was still there,
But it wasn't expressed.

They both cared deeply,
But life didn't have the same plans.

Destiny was going to take them away from each other,
And they couldn't do anything about it.

As time passed, their aspirations became obsessions,
Love was taken for granted.

MEANINGFUL LIFE

They both wanted a meaningful life,
Life and love had lost their colors.

Both of them wanted to be successful,
But the cost was their love.

She wanted to make art primary,
Everything else was secondary.

He wanted to earn a lot,
Love couldn't earn his bread for him.

He yearned for luxuries,
Luxuries which were not his necessities.

In the beginning, she was his life,
But life had changed its meaning.

The plan to break off was actually his,
She just obeyed diligently.

She was heart-broken when he left
She had to surrender to art.

Jaydeep Khot

He became a work robot,
There were no feelings left.

Some days, he remembered her,
And sometimes, a tear fell from his eyes.

They had both wanted a meaningful life,
And that was what they got.

27

FALL APART

They were falling apart,
The friendship was also gone.

She cried silently,
He also didn't raise a noise.

Both missed each other,
But did nothing.

He thought about her before sleeping,
She thought about him after she woke up.

They were together somewhere,
In a world where love never died.

She believed in his abilities,
He trusted her skills.

They didn't want to ruin each other,
But they had ruined their love.

There were no memories left to remember,
No future to imagine.

Their hearts had turned to stone,
Ambition drove them instead of love.

They had fallen apart,
Barely remembering each other.

The two parts of the same heart which fit perfectly,
Were no longer hearts at all.

PART 2

THE STRUGGLE

DAILY LIFE

Their respective lives continued,
They were complete strangers now.

Their happiness didn't last long,
The color faded soon.

Their life became mundane,
It lacked meaning.

They tried to go out with other people,
But found nobody worth their time.

He thought about her,
She thought about him.

They weren't together,
It was the bitter truth.

He called her but she was busy,
She called back but he was busy.

No matter how hard they tried,
Nothing in the world seemed to work out.

They didn't have time to live,
Their life was meant to be lived together.

She prayed for him every day,
He remembered her in his dreams.

Their daily lives were a mess,
But their past gave them some hope.

They did not have each other,
But they wished to be together.

Their love was eternal,
They wanted to return to it.

HIS AMBITION

He wanted to reach the top,
He didn't care how.

He was the best in the business
And he worked hard to stay there,

He became inhumane,
Ruthless was what his co-workers called him.

He was venting out his frustration,
The frustration of not being with her.

His life was boring,
His ambition was all that remained.

Typing for endless hours,
Making PowerPoint presentations.

His heart belonged with her,
But he buried it in his work.

He wished for her to be back in his life,
But he knew, she was too far away now.

He was worthless without her,
She was his entire life.

His ambition was meaningless,
There was nothing without her.

He worked very hard,
But his mind constantly wandered.

He had reached the top,
But it was lonely without her.

HER AMBITION

Her heart was in art,
She wanted to be the most revered artist in the world.

But her painting lacked love,
Her passion was incomplete.

This frustrated her,
Her brush lost its magic.

She dreamt about being number one,
But she was nowhere near.

Her life came to a stop,
She felt depressed and alone.

She missed him very much,
But couldn't express it.

She tried hard to improve,
She poured her heart out.

It was of no use,
Love was gone, her passion was gone.

She wanted him back,
But knew she couldn't have him.

Her soul was restless,
Searching for true love.

Her magic had faded,
Her passion no longer existed.

His love was all she wanted,
He was the best thing that had ever happened.

Her dreams were of him,
But her life had totally changed.

There was no hope,
And it was very hard for her to cope.

MISSING HER

He missed her every day,
Thought about her every moment.

His life revolved around her,
He just wanted to see her smile.

Her smile was beautiful,
The most beautiful thing he had ever seen.

There was no life without her,
He was dead inside.

Her thoughts kept him occupied,
Days went by like seconds.

He wondered how she was doing,
Was she happy or sad?

He wanted her to be happy,
No matter what the cost was.

He met her friend to find out more,
She didn't know much.

Life was a tragedy,
All he needed was a remedy.

He was really ill,
Love was the only medicine.

It was time to act,
If something had to happen it would.

He needed love,
Love which only she could provide.

She could come back, if she wanted to,
But the question was did she want it too?

MISSING HIM

She felt betrayed by her own self,
Her passion had betrayed her.

He was the person on her mind,
Not her art.

Things weren't as they were supposed to be,
They were falling apart.

His meaningful talks and charming personality,
Returned to her in her dreams.

She was constantly thinking about him,
Nothing else would distract her.

She was a different person with him,
Today she didn't know her own self.

Upset, one day, she called him.
He quickly answered.

In no time they got talking,
They connected again in one go.

They felt like they were back to life,
Revived from the dead.

Their happiness knew no limits,
They were continuously smiling.

Life had brought back the hope,
Which had vanished long back.

Love had won again,
It was time to rejoice.

THE MEETING

Their meeting was going to be eternal,
Both would remember it forever.

They looked at each other,
In that most awaited moment;

It was a reunion of their souls,
Never to be taken for granted again.

They didn't speak at all,
Words couldn't describe it.

They held hands,
Their hearts reconnected.

Their eyes met,
Their souls were one, once again.

They had suffered once,
But it was worth it.

The love they now shared,
It was something out of the world.

But it was time to depart,
They had spent a lot of time together.

He had to rush for office,
She had her art class.

When he was about to leave,
She held his hand firmly.

He smiled at her,
She looked nervous.

Love was a complicated affair,
They knew it best.

After all they went through,
They didn't want to lose each other again.

FLASHBACK

They relived each memory,
The same way it happened originally.

They visited her favorite coffee shop,
His favorite clothing store.

They had the time of their lives,
Love had brought back the joy in them.

This was a different stage for them,
Their cloud had a silver lining.

They talked for hours on the phone,
Giving each other all minute details.

Their love story was back on track,
This was a blessing, after the horrible hurricane.

Considering themselves lucky,
They now focused only on positivity.

The past was dark,
But the future was bright.

They had gone through a lot,
But the time was now better.

What happened yesterday made them value today,
And taking care of what the future held.

CAN'T WAIT

It was time to tell their parents,
The story of their love.

They couldn't wait anymore,
They wanted to tie the knot.

They were excited,
But nervous at the same time.

The thrill was back in their relationship,
And they really loved it.

Their plan was perfect,
They were going to tell their parents soon.

It was his dad's birthday,
When he told them.

She was present there,
And couldn't stop blushing.

His parents hugged her,
His mother had tears in her eyes.

She told her parents during their anniversary,
It was a joyful event.

He attended the event,
Her father shook his hand and called him 'son'.

They were really happy,
Their love was magical.

Wedding dates were fixed,
The engagement was done.

Preparations started in all force,
They couldn't wait anymore.

THE BRIGHT FUTURE

The future was promising,
It had hope like never before.

It was incredible,
Their families were now one.

Even before the wedding,
Everybody was happy together.

They thought about all they went through,
What they were now.

Life had showed them the path,
It was a miracle.

They were going to get married,
Soon to become a certified couple.

They deserved this, after all their sorrows,
It was their day.

The stage was well decorated,
Flowers everywhere the eyes could see.

The groom was well suited,
All ready to get married.

Finally, the bride arrived,
She was the most beautiful girl on earth.

Wearing a cream white dress,
Her cheeks turned pink as she blushed.

They accepted each other as their soul mates,
It was a lovely day—that history could never forget.

FINALLY TOGETHER

Their stars were in the right place,
So were their lives together.

Happily married,
The sign on their house read.

It was time for a vacation,
Popularly known as honeymoon.

London was his choice,
But New York was her command.

They were soon in Manhattan,
He was handling her shopping bags.

She was a shopaholic,
He was her admirer turned lover.

She continued her shopping spree,
He continued admiring her beauty and enthusiasm.

He hardly saw the sights,
He could only see her.

She could hardly see the clothes she bought,
She could only see him.

They were perfect together,
God had blessed them with love.

Within a week of coming back,
She found that she was pregnant.

Their love was going to be born,
It was going to leave a mark on the world.

They celebrated the arrival of a new family member,
With a small house party.

PART 3
THEIR WORLD

CARE

She was born,
Their first child in the family.

The source of all joy,
Prettier than the most beautiful flower.

She was very delicate,
They hoped that nothing hurt her.

She was blessed to have them,
They were delighted to have her.

A beautiful angel,
Was what everybody called her.

Fair and chubby,
She was a sight to behold.

He cut down on his work,
She gave up painting.

Their child was topmost priority,
Nothing could replace her.

Suddenly, she fell sick,
They were really scared.

They prayed to the almighty for her health,
Medicines and help was bought,

Her condition was worsened,
They didn't know what had cursed them.

They took extreme care of her,
It was up to them to make her survive.

BIRTH OF JOY

She was well again,
Their daughter was recovering.

It called for an occasion,
One to be cherished forever.

They called in relatives,
From both the sides of the family.

Their daughter was dressed up,
She looked like a beautiful princess.

It was a moment to rejoice.
Everybody seemed at peace.

Their angel was safe,
What else could they need?

They cut the cake,
It was strawberry flavored—her favorite.

The area was decorated with balloons,
Of different colors.

The angel smiled,
It was her first.

They captured it on camera,
The picture would be engraved in their hearts.

Everybody gave her gifts,
She was a blessed baby,

Their family was complete,
Nothing could break their unity.

They wished the best for their baby,
Because she was the best in the world.

FIRST WALK

Their angel turned out to be healthy,
Her cuteness was one of a kind.

On days he came home late,
They both stayed awake for him.

The family slept together,
Stayed together.

On day, they woke up,
And saw their angel walk.

It was a marvelous sight,
They could never forget it.

Her little feet touched the ground,
They marked her footsteps there.

It was an achievement for the family.
And it was unforgettable.

As they hugged her,
They heard her laugh.

It was melodious,
Nobody could ever replicate it.

Life was an adventure,
Every day brought something new.

All they wanted was her happiness,
She was the luckiest girl in the world.

Her eyes were deep blue,
Showing the depth of her soul.

God had been kind to them,
They couldn't be more content.

EDUCATION

She was ready for school,
Ready to be a model citizen.

They wanted her to learn,
But not only to earn.

A new phase had started for her,
But she had difficulties,

She wasn't a bright child.
Less than average, the world said

But she was artistic,
Just like her mother.

She had the skills,
And they encouraged her.

She grew up to be smart,
In her own way.

Her beauty complemented her,
Her personality was unique.

She went on to be successful,
Successful in her own way.

She was happy,
That was what helped her survive.

She was brave,
She had the courage to be different.

They loved her,
They let her be herself.

HEALTH

His wife fell ill,
There was something terribly wrong.

They couldn't understand the reason,
All the doctors had given up hope.

God was the only hope,
All they could do was pray.

She had high fever,
It just wouldn't go down.

Day by day, she became depressed,
Darkness had surrounded her.

She was sick,
Physically as well as mentally.

He wanted to see her smile,
Wanted to fill her life with joy.

He tried a lot,
But all his attempts failed.

He felt miserable,
But he had to be strong.

He bought flowers,
Her favorite ones.

It brought a smile on her face,
A sign of hope resurfaced.

Their daughter could understand,
The situation was serious.

She tried to play with her mother,
To make her happy.

The touch of a daughter,
Was the medicine for her sick mother.

DISCIPLINE

Their angel was getting out of hand,
Nothing could hurt them more.

Her art was just an excuse,
She was giving in to addiction.

She was drinking underage.
They wanted to help her,

But she enjoyed it,
She was not ashamed.

They tried to convince her,
But she wanted to have fun.

Late night parties,
Became her daily routine.

She thought her life was complicated,
But she was making it so.

Alcoholism was bad,
That's what her parents told her.

She didn't care,
It made her cool.

Her mother cried,
The night she didn't come home.

The next day she returned,
With tears in her eyes.

She understood her fault,
It is never too late.

They forgave her,
She was their own blood after all.

ENJOYMENT

Years after the wait,
A son was born to them.

She was an elder sister,
She felt responsible now.

A girl, and then a boy,
They were really blessed.

They remembered their times,
How complicated life was.

Today, everything was fine,
Only because of the almighty divine.

Her brother was lucky to have her,
She now had company to play with.

Her life was filled with joy,
She could do anything for him,

He changed her,
She became a better person.

Taking the role of an elder sister,
She became his godmother.

Nothing could trouble him,
Not even a small insect.

It was a time of enjoyment,
He had made their lives better.

TIME FOR SCHOOL

He had started school,
His days were really interesting.

Unlike his sister, he was smart,
He was at the top in his class.

Be it sports or studies,
He was the best.

Popular among her friends,
He was envied a lot.

Charming in looks,
He resembled his father.

Although, he was successful,
He was humble and kind.

He helped the needy,
He was never greedy.

Everybody admired him,
His life was a roller coaster ride,

He stood up for good,
He was a nice person at heart.

His parents were proud of him,
His sister always had his back.

The day he wasn't well,
Everybody would be upset.

The day he was fine,
Everybody would be happy.

Such was the love he shared,
The eternal love of his family.

25 YEARS TOGETHER

The couple completed 25 years,
25 years of eternal love.

Their daughter was now to be married,
Their son was an energetic teenager.

Life was beautiful,
A memorable story.

They had a small celebration,
Where they cut a big cake,

It resembled their heart,
The heart which was a part of their souls.

They danced gracefully,
Their children admired them.

The old man was well suited,
The old lady was well dressed.

They were the perfect couple,
Their children had tears in their eyes.

A lot of pictures were clicked,
It was meant to be put on the walls.

The day was a memorable one,
One where they relived their youth.

Time flied,
They couldn't believe it.

They wanted to live each day again,
It went by too fast for them.

Their love story was irreplaceable,
It gave their lives meaning.

EXPECTATIONS

As parents, they had expectations,
Expectations from their kids.

They were reasonable,
But were taken as a burden.

It was a gift,
But taken as a curse.

They wanted their kids to be responsible,
But only if their kids understood.

After all that they did for them,
This was expected from them.

They told their parents things,
Things which were difficult to hear.

Their heart pained,
It was something their souls couldn't bear.

Their life was shattered,
While trying to make their kid's lives.

Their kids didn't value it,
The value of their concern.

Their love was misunderstood,
It was mistaken for control.

Their kids wanted to be free,
So they separated from them.

They didn't even say goodbye,
It was hard for them.

They wanted their kids to smile,
Their welfare was their only wish.

PART 4

ANOTHER LOVE STORY

THEIR EYES MET

He was young,
He couldn't help falling for her beauty.

Their eyes met,
And it started another love story.

She was a beautiful girl,
With a confident personality.

He was smart,
But a little unsure of approaching her.

He gathered courage,
Took his first step.

She smiled nervously,
He smiled back.

He hesitated to say hello.
But he would never regret it.

She was glad,
She knew he would come to talk.

They had common friends,
Friends who were dear to them.

They knew their intentions,
They tried to help them.

Both of them were shy,
They were still young.

But they wanted to be together,
No matter what happened.

Their eyes met,
Now, their hearts had to.

ACQUAINTANCE

They knew each other,
But not too well.

He liked her,
But didn't know if he loved her.

She admired him,
Found him cute.

His heart beats grew faster,
When she passed by.

She had a melodious voice,
He loved listening to it.

She worked hard in her rehearsals,
She wanted to achieve great heights.

He was good in sports,
A master of the high jump.

All the girls cheered for him,
She did too.

She envied the girls who talked to him,
She was afraid of showing her emotions.

She didn't want to be vulnerable,
She was known to be strong.

Love weakened her,
That was what she thought.

But this was going to be her strength,
She just wasn't aware of it yet.

CHILDISH LOVE

They were in love,
But their love was immature.

He tried to impress her,
She pretended to be flattered.

She was his dream,
He never wanted to wake up.

She realized that she loved him,
But didn't know how to express it.

She was extremely delicate,
He didn't want to hurt her.

He knew about her,
A lot more than she knew about herself.

He was a friend first,
A friend who could do anything for her.

She was impressed by him,
By his personality and attitude.

She had always wanted to be in love,
But when the time came, she hesitated.

They wanted to make their love eternal,
But were afraid that it would never last.

They were young and stupid,
Mistakes were made.

They didn't care much,
But it would affect their future.

Individually, they were the great,
Together, they were the best.

Their childish love was taking a step ahead,
They welcomed it with open arms.

To become eternal love needed to stand the test of time,
Time which they did not have.

HINTS

He gave her hints,
Hints, that he loved her.

She received them well,
But ignored them intentionally.

She did it mischievously,
He was aware of her mischief.

He acted like he didn't care,
But he cared deeply.

Whenever she was sad,
He gave her a shoulder to cry on.

He defended her,
Against all the bad in the world.

He wiped her tears,
With his handkerchief.

She was happy with him,
But didn't want to commit.

They were more than in love,
They were soul mates.

Their relationship didn't have a name,
But it was above all.

Their bond was sacred,
It was purer that ever.

She hugged him,
Every time they met.

He hugged back,
With the most amazing smile.

His hints were fruitful,
She was now ready for friendship.

FRIENDSHIP

A friendship like no other,
Was established between them.

Soon to be lovers,
They first tested the waters.

From acquaintances to friends,
It was a fruitful journey.

A journey they would cherish,
For years to come.

People didn't like this,
The concept of lovers being friends.

They thought it was deceptive,
With no destination to meet.

But the love birds were content,
They didn't want anything else.

They knew about their love,
There was no necessity to prove it.

Their life was beautiful,
Their relationship had a name.

Their bond was a symbol of togetherness,
That's what they said.

Happiness knew no limits,
They loved each other's company,

They chose to ignore what people said,
Their love was above this all.

Their friendship came before their love,
A bond which would last forever.

THE OUTING

They planned an outing,
Just the two of them.

They wanted to spend quality time.
In the midst of nature,

It was a picnic,
In a beautiful garden;

Full of greenery,
And flowers and birds,

The sunflowers stood up with all its might,
Radiating happiness.

The birds chirped,
The songs were music to the ears.

The couple talked about life,
The meanings attached to it.

They talked about ambitions,
Dreams which didn't let them sleep at night.

Their hearts finally met,
Now, their love was one.

They would do anything for each other,
Only death could do them apart.

They enjoyed the scenery,
And each other's company

He didn't ever want to leave her,
But he had to one day.

She was unaware of the situation,
But she would know it someday.

HELP

There was an accident – she fell down,
A hard stone hit her head,

She was bleeding,
She required urgent help.

Nobody was nearby,
He was helpless.

He ran everywhere to find aid,
But it was of no use.

He picked her up,
And walked to the nearest hospital.

He was drained,
She was critical.

The doctors saved her,
It was a miracle.

A miracle which he made happen,
With his determination.

He gave her life,
She would always treasure it.

Life was meaningful,
All because of him.

She lived each day to the fullest,
Keeping him in her memories.

He was her life,
She wanted to live.

They were inseparable,
Only time could reveal their destiny.

TRUST

She caught him with someone else,
She was devastated.

Her trust was broken,
She could never love again.

He tried to reason with her,
He told her, they were just friends.

But her soul knew the truth,
It caused her heart to ache.

She didn't pick his calls,
Or reply to his messages.

He was not given an opportunity to explain,
Though he tried his best to.

Love was gone,
Her life had lost color,

Her love was eternal,
But her lover wasn't.

She felt betrayed,
He was now a stranger again,

She couldn't trust again,
Her heart was broken.

But she had the courage,
To admit her shortcomings.

She would stand tall,
In spite of her failures.

BONDING

She found love again,
Eternal love.

Love in her parents,
Who loved her till death.

Their love was real,
They cared for her.

They had warned her about him,
She hadn't listened.

Today, she understood,
What they had warned about.

She felt stupid,
She should have listened.

Her parents didn't worry,
They were happy that she understood.

They didn't taunt her,
They celebrated her freedom.

They gave her immense love,
She felt blessed to have parents like them.

They assured her that they would find somebody,
Somebody who loved her.

She didn't mind,
She was proud of her mistake.

She learnt from it,
It made her a better decision maker.

Her life was now clear,
She knew what she wanted to do.

She wanted to take care of her parents,
They didn't have much time left.

TOGETHER

Her family was complete,
She now knew its meaning.

They were together,
Nothing could break them apart.

She was finding love,
Love which was already there.

She couldn't be more content,
Her love belonged at the feet of her parents.

She worshipped them,
Showered them with eternal happiness.

They couldn't believe their luck,
They had won their daughter back.

She was better than ever before,
Heartbreak had made her wise.

She now valued true love,
She could easily distinguish it from false.

Betrayal was never going to touch her again,
She was with the right people.

People who cared for her,
Loved her with everything they had.

His memories were erased from her mind,
Her love for him was gone.

She was independent,
Her decisions were now more calculated.

Every time she did something,
She thought about her parents first.

Her family was happy,
They didn't want anything more.

Their lives were filled with a magical love,
They were now together forever.

PART 5

OLD-AGE CHRONICLES

GROWING WEAK AND STRONG

They were now in their seventies,
Their knees were weak.

They could barely walk,
Their kids were no longer with them.

But they had no regrets,
They were satisfied.

Satisfied with their life,
Satisfied with their relationship.

Their love lasted forever,
It would even after death.

They were physically weak,
But spiritually strong.

Life treated them the way they wanted,
What else could they ask for?

Their kids were gone,
They had made them into good people.

He gave her a rose,
A rose which was the prettiest of all.

She gave him a greeting card,
Which she had painted by herself.

They were each other's strengths,
No weakness could harm them.

They grew together,
They were inseparable.

Generations would tell their story,
They had created a mark in history.

A NEW GENERATION

A new thought process,
A modern generation.

New fashion,
A different style of living.

It was unusual,
Yet acceptable.

The change was here,
They had to agree.

Their kids had grown up,
And grown apart from them.

They tried their best,
But couldn't stop them.

They were free birds now,
Nothing could ever trap them.

They loved them,
But their meaning of love was different.

The new generation's love was materialistic,
Something which could be easily bought.

Only if they could understand the true meaning,
Their love could be noble.

They wanted things,
Things which were available in the market.

Their parents could offer them much more,
But they failed to understand,

They forgot their parents,
The parents who had spent their entire life on them.

Parents are a form of god,
A god they no longer worshipped.

ADAPTING

They had to move on,
Adjust to the current scenario.

Their kids were gone,
Their absence was felt.

There was nothing they could do about it,
They had to accept that fact.

They remembered how their kids grew,
Unique and different.

They took proper care of them,
They did everything could.

Still their kids left them,
When they needed them the most.

What if they had aborted them?
They would have never existed.

It was a sin,
But it would lesser their pain.

They were becoming selfish,
But so did their kids.

They felt depressed,
They didn't have a hand to hold.

They had taught them,
To be responsible,

But they ran away,
When they had to take responsibility.

Had they been wrong in their upbringing,
They wondered.

The answer was a clear no,
That was all they could conclude.

They had to adapt to the situation,
They had no choice.

TRUTH OF LIFE

She was getting sick,
She had very less time,

He went to the best of the doctors,
But there was no major help.

Her time was coming near,
He wanted to avoid it.

The consequence of living was death,
He had to accept it.

She had to live for him,
She knew this deep inside.

He couldn't live without her,
She was the only person he had.

She started losing memory,
Slowly she couldn't recognize him.

This saddened him,
But he didn't leave her side.

He was with her,
Till her very end.

He didn't want her to go,
But it was inevitable.

DEMISE

She was gone,
Gone far away from him.

He wanted to bring her back,
But he couldn't.

He could give away anything,
Only to live a day again with her.

But it wasn't possible,
She was no more.

She had taken his heart,
He had no life left in him.

He had no emotions left,
He stopped smiling.

Her demise had shattered him,
He was affected deeply.

Life was depressing,
Nobody could help him now.

They had promised to be together,
She broke her promise.

He still loved her,
Nobody could replace her.

His children were back,
But they were too late.

He was just breathing,
He was spiritually somewhere else.

His children tried to bring him back,
But they could never find him.

FOREVER IN HIS MEMORIES

She was immortal,
Immortal in his memories.

Each day, he remembered her,
Like she was still living with him.

Her smile, her laughter, her charm,
He recalled everything.

She was his love,
And he could never forget her.
He would join her soon,
He was just waiting for that day.

His heart belonged to her,
Nobody else could own it.

But she was gone,
Gone to a place of peace.

He counted the days,
The days seemed like years.

He missed her,
It was now his regular job.

He wanted to be with her,
Forever in his memories.

THEY MEET IN HEAVEN

The wait was over,
He finally met her.

She appeared as an angel,
He hugged her,

Standing on the clouds,
They smiled at each other.

They were finally free,
Free from earthly bondage.

They held hands,
And looked at the sky.

The angels blessed them,
The cupid didn't need to strike its arrow.

Heaven was complete,
The love story had a happy ending.

They were together,
After a very long time.

They were on the top of the world,
Nothing could separate them.

She was waiting for him too,
The heavenly angels told him.

They could see their kids from above,
Their kids had realized their mistakes.

They could not amend it,
But only regret it.

They were in Heaven,
Their love was now eternal.

THEIR MARK ON THE WORLD

Their kids lived on,
Their stories were told for generations.

Their kids became responsible,
Their last wish was fulfilled.

They were happy in heaven,
They wanted nothing more.

Seeing their kids working,
What else could they wish for?

They had spent their lives together,
Now they were back again.

Even death couldn't do them apart,
They were indeed blessed.

Their love had won,
Time couldn't harm them.

They would be born again,
To give the world another love story.

They taught people to love,
Love which was selfless.

They cared deeply,
Without asking for anything in return.

Could they ever witness such a love again?
Was the question asked by generations to come.

Their mark on the world was prominent,
An example which was unforgettable.

They smiled looking down from the heaven,
At others who struggled for love.

ETERNAL LOVE- 1

True love is not easy,
One needs to fight for it.

It seems joyful,
But the past is full of pain.

It has to stand the test of time,
A lot of patience is essential.

Love needs to be true,
Materialism is not important.

When the other person is happy,
You are happy.

When the other person is sad,
You are sad.

Such is eternal love,
Their mood affects yours.

Expectations exist,
But they are not mandatory.

Love doesn't come with conditions,
They may or may not be satisfied.

You need to believe in your love,
In order to get it.

There is no reason to prove your love to the world,
It is implied.

You must be brave to love,
It takes real courage to love with all your heart.

Do whatever you can,
Because love is about giving.

If you receive love,
Be grateful.

If you are loved back,
Thank god; not everyone is as blessed as you are.

ETERNAL LOVE- 2

One-sided love is painful,
It is often misunderstood.

Love should not be forced,
Then it is not true love.

Love must give joy,
Not negative vibes.

If it is used as a controlling tool,
It is obsession and not love.

Obsession is harmful,
It does no good.

Love is free,
It should never be controlled.

For love to be eternal,
You have to let go.

There should be no barriers,
It is not a prison.

Authority does not come in love,
But duty does.

You are responsible in love,
But there is no compulsion.

Once there is compulsion,
It is a punishment, not love.

Love needs to be given with an open heart,
As well as an open mind.

Do not hate somebody else,
It will only affect your well being.

When you are cursed,
Bless them in return.

Criticism is a form of concern,
Concern is an off-shoot of eternal love.

Poet:
Jaydeep Khot